A Stubborn Dog: GG

This Blog Book Is Dedicated To Everyone
That Has Or Wanted To Have A Dog.

Preface

I'm Anita Powell, the author of A Stubborn Dog: GG. I hope you enjoy reading this little slice of my life; a series of blog posts make up this story from the time I got GG at 8 weeks to present. The story gives you information on what and what not to do with a dog. It also shows what can happen in a relationship when one person is a dog lover and the other a nonlover. When you see repeats, it is because of the time in between me writing a post. It is funny and heartwarming all rolled up together. It's a book of unconditional love. While this is about me and GG, it is also a love story, thanks to GG.

Post 1

The Beginning

I was just out of a relationship and I hated - I mean literally hated - coming home to emptiness. I had coworkers who were always talking about dogs, so with my hating coming home to emptiness, and them filling my head with the wonders of pet ownership, I decided to get a dog. I had just moved into a new apartment, and I didn't know that pets were forbidden. This was something I didn't have to consider when I moved into the apartment because I didn't think about getting a dog. After months of going back and forth, and seeing the people that lived across from me with a cat, I decided, 'well, if they can have a cat, I can have a dog.' I did inquire with management, who told me no pets. I think there was a double standard there; they could rationalize cats but not dogs. I wasn't hearing it. I was sitting at work one day a week before Thanksgiving, bored crazy and I decided: today, I'm getting my dog. A coworker told me where to go, which was way out in Brooklyn, NY. I lived way up in New Jersey, close to the Poconos. I was not to be deterred by distance. I took the train to Brooklyn, NY. I didn't know what I was looking for, just a small dog that didn't shed all over the place. There were a lot of people looking at dogs and a lot of dogs looking for a new home. I saw this group of Shih Tzus, all different colors and so small. I was in love, but which one? The one I chose ran to me when the owner of the store took her out. I was in love; then the bad news came. She had a hernia, and they'd take care of it, but I wanted my dog now and I didn't want to make that trip to again. I went back to the small group of Shih Tzus and picked another. When the store owner let her out, she walked in the opposite direction of me. Stubborn; I'll take her! I purchased a carrier that looked like a purse for the long trip back to New Jersey. She slept most of the way to her new home. We finally arrived at my car after what seemed like hours. I was tired and I was hoping so was she. I hadn't prepared at all for this dog. I had no food, no training pads, and no permission for a dog. It was dark and she was sleep. I ran into the store thank god it wasn't crowded because I had to leave her in the carrier while I picked up few things for her. Finally, home. I let her out the carrier so she could get familiar with her new home. She peed on the floor, and almost fell down the stairs that lead to the front door. I was tired, and the reason I got the dog went out the window now that I had to cleanup pee and babyproof the stairs.

Post 2

Home Sweet Home

The problems start mounting when you make impulsive decisions, as you are usually unprepared for the results. I was very unprepared, and not very knowledgeable about dogs. I grew up where people had mutts for dogs – you gave him a bone and went about your business. But high-end dogs take some care and thought. What kind of food should she eat, wet or dry? Do you know how many kinds of dog food there are? What about shots? You know what, let's stop right here – I haven't even given her a name. The next day I had more pee to clean up; does this dog do anything but pee, I thought? I gave her the food I grabbed at the store the night before and sat trying to figure out a name. I wanted it to be easy and a reflection of her personality, whilst to be honest at this point, I knew nothing about her. I thought maybe I'd name her DEE, but nope, that won't do – my mom would kill me for naming a dog after her! Then I thought DD... Nope, still too close to my mother's name. I went through the entire alphabet in my head, putting two letters together. Finally, I decided on GG. No Gigi for her, just two letters, easy to remember. I was a proud mama, I managed to give my dog a name. The next problem to tackle was buying more dog food and training pads. I couldn't take her with me, because I wasn't supposed to have a dog – so what was I to do? I had no choice but to go, she needed things. As I was leaving for my quick run to the store a Cesar dog food commercial came on. I stopped in my tracks and just stared at the television, as if I had never seen this commercial before. This time was different, GG needed food and the Cesar dog was cute. I went to the store so fast you'd think it was a matter of life and death. It was obvious I was a proud mama with all the toys I bought her. I just hoped that nobody behind me in line knew where I lived. I rushed all the way from the checkout line to my car just grinning. Well, that smile got wiped right off my face when I got home... GG had pooped on the floor, torn up a training pad and dragged my shoes out of the bedroom. How can one little dog do so much in 15 minutes? I was furious, and she got her first and only spanking with a newspaper. I'd learned a few things from the dog lovers at my job. They said to crate train her. A crate is basically a cage. Crate training involves putting your dog in and out of a cage for a time period until the dog thinks of the crate as a safe place. People usually will put their dog in the crate when they are out for work, so their house isn't a mess when they got home. There are some who use crates for their dogs at night for sleeping. The dog usually doesn't mind, because to them it's a place of comfort. Crate training can take days or weeks depending on the dog. It seemed inhuman to me because of the number of hours I wasn't home. GG and I practiced me going out and staying for different amounts of time all weekend. I had to go work in NYC. I left at 4 in the morning and didn't get home until 5. I had forgotten all about this when I impulsively got GG. I never considered that she might be lonely being home alone for that many hours. I do realize now it was selfish... There was also the issue of noise. I had downstairs neighbors and I know with those thin walls the floors were probably not much better. I wondered, did they hear her running or see her little head, looking out of the patio door? I was just glad her bark was weak, and the neighbors were nice.

Post 3

Oh Boy!!

The first day back to work was stressful, and that's an understatement. I worried that GG might cry being home alone, or that our training pad sessions hadn't gone as well as I thought. The commute I took to work was at least 2hrs each way, so there was plenty of time for her to get into mischief. I had read online that giving your pet an article of clothing would help reduce their anxiety. I gave her one of my socks to hopefully pacify her. I couldn't take her out because it was dark at the time I left for work. I barely wanted to go out myself at 4am to go to the bus, so I knew she wouldn't want to go out. I can honestly say that was one stressful long day, not knowing what I was coming home to.

When I got out of my car in front of my building, I looked both ways before I got out. I didn't want to get ambushed by neighbors or rental office personnel. I gingerly walked to the door, and put my ear against it, "Ahhhhh... nothing." No noise whatsoever. I opened the door and who did I see, but GG. Let me explain. There were about 15 steps to climb to get into the apartment. I picked her up and hugged her. I wondered how long she had been there. I can't imagine such a small dog getting down all of those stairs without hurting herself. I did a once over of her body, to make sure that she wasn't hurt anywhere, and got our dinner.

I was exhausted. Between the commute and the stress, I was ready to relax and go to bed; 3am comes very early. Well, GG had other plans, like playing and running all over the apartment. The neighbors downstairs must have wondered whether I lost my mind with all that tapping on the floor. What choice did I have but to throw toys for her to fetch, hoping she would tire out? (Which was not happening.) After fetch, it was rubbing her, and I must have fallen asleep in the middle of that, because I remember her little bark that caused me to jump up. No, there can't be any barking. None whatsoever. Doesn't this dog ever get tired? It must be the dog food, it must have some energizer ingredient in it, I thought to myself. I was exhausted by the time she finished her night of seeing what my breaking point was. This nighttime playtime had to go. I would never be able to go to work if this was going to be her nightly routine.

I thought Shih Tzus were lap dogs, which meant that they only wanted to lay in your lap and sleep, not run around like a maniac. I had to get her outside to burn up some of her energy. That was a challenge, because, again, I was not supposed to have a dog. I had to figure out how to get her out the door at a time when people were coming in from work. She also had to be quiet and not draw attention to us. I also had to figure out where to take her where no one from my development would know me. This was as bad as a robber making plans to rob a bank. I had to go over every detail in my head.

Post 4

Secret Agent

I was like agent 007 from the television show Get Smart. I did all kinds of crazy things to keep her from being seen, such as pretending she was a baby. I would wrap her in a blanket and hold her like a baby. When someone would start walking in my direction, I'd just say "bad cold." That was enough to keep people away. You know kids though: that was harder – they didn't care about colds. I used a different approach. With clenched teeth and a smile, I shook my head to say "no." It worked, that's all I know. The other method of getting GG out was putting her in a gym bag. I must say, this turned out to be the best way. I guess people thought I worked out seven days a week, because people would see me in and out, with my gym bag. There were hiccups along the way that were nerve-wracking for me. GG still wanted to run and play in the house, no matter how long I kept her out. She never seemed to get tired. It got so bad that at times, I would sit in my car because I just couldn't deal with her playing. Yes, I would be sitting in my car listening to music trying to get the energy to confront her. Was I a bad parent? I didn't care. I was away from home 12 to 13 hours a day. I commuted to New York from near the Poconos. I was being kept up way past my bedtime. I felt like a walking zombie. Pep talk time, Anita: you wanted a dog, because you didn't like coming home to an empty house. Well, GG filled all the criteria. I had to get it together and drudge back upstairs. The next bad experience I had was giving her a chicken bone. Remember, I said people I grew up with gave a dog a bone and kept it moving, well, that's a big no-go. She was so sick; I was up all night with her. I thought to myself: "this is great – I have a dog for a few months and I'm killing her." I was so stressed. She looked so pitiful and there was nothing I could do. I didn't have any of the dog-lovers from my job's telephone numbers, so I couldn't call anyone that I thought might know what to do. I had to find a vet and quick. I didn't care how far I had to go, or how much it was going to cost. I just wanted her fixed. Thank god for the internet. I found a vet about 10 minutes away. The vet gave her fluids and a shot and told me to buy Pepto Bismol. I had to ask her to repeat the directions because I was now wondering if this vet, had graduated from medical school. I reluctantly and I mean reluctantly bought and gave GG the Pepto Bismol. It took about two days before she was back to her playful self. I was so happy to throw her toy across the room for her fetch.

The days went by with our routine of sneaking her out and playing. I was still exhausted, but I no longer had to give myself pep talks, or sit in my car to get away from her. Things were going along fine until smoke alarm changing time.

Post 5

Smoke Alarm: Argh

Let me say right now, I'm all for smoke alarms, however the smoke alarm in my apartment caused me a lot of problems. I'm just going to reiterate there was a no-pet policy in this development. Why did I get a dog? Simple. I saw people out of my balcony window that had cats. I reasoned a cat is as much of a pet as a dog, so that's it. Right or wrong, that's how I reasoned. I also hated coming home to an empty house. You know, when you're used to coming home to a person or a pet and that goes away, sometimes you just don't get over that emptiness. Things were going as well as they could with me sneaking around with GG. I don't know if I mentioned this, but it was around Thanksgiving when I got her, so it was cold out. This was another thing I didn't consider when I got this bright idea for a dog. She had to go out for my sanity. It was easier to deal with her "I want to play because I've been alone all day!" by taking her out for a few minutes. This meant coats, which meant dressing and undressing her. No fun, she hated clothes, and to this day, she still hates putting on clothes.

Okay, smoke alarm, you know how every year usually a housing development will send someone to change the smoke alarm batteries? I had a notice on my door one day that someone would be coming in to change my smoke alarm batteries. I panicked. Wouldn't you? I had to think. They only gave you about a week's notice. I knew I had to go into my 007 mode to not be found out for having a pet. I stayed home from work, that was no problem. The problem was that it was January and snowing outside. I couldn't go out with her even to sit in the car. Well, maybe I could have, now that I'm thinking about. I could have cleaned the snow off the car and turned on the heat, and we could have sat in the car which was parked right outside my building. We could have watched the worker go in the apartment and come out. I just didn't think of that then. What did I do? I put GG in her carrier, which I placed on the other side of the bed and closed the bedroom door. I turned music on and up loud. The smoke alarm was right outside the bedroom door so when he put up his ladder to change the smoke alarm batteries, I stood right there and started some stupid conversation. I can't remember what it was. I could hear GG barking. Thank God her bark was not loud. The smoke alarm guy would periodically look at the door, and I'd just keep talking. It only lasted about five or six minutes, but that was a nerve-racking experience. I was so happy when he left that I took GG and threw toys from one end of the living room to the other. I was so happy we hadn't been found out. The doorbell rang and I wondered, 'Who that can be?' People don't visit me without calling first. I picked up GG and practically threw her in the bedroom. No carrier this time, I just put her in there and closed the door. It was him back for me to sign a paper to say he'd changed the batteries in the smoke alarm. I will always believe he came back trying to catch me in the wrong. I didn't let him in because there was no reason that he needed to enter the apartment. I stood in the doorway and signed. Wow! That was close. I got away with the battery change that year.

Post 6

Dating

Things were routine after the smoke alarm incident. I would park as close to the building as possible, run in, and get into my 007 mode. I hadn't done any dating since I had gotten GG; she took up most of my time. I got up at 3am and didn't get home until 530 or 6pm. It maybe wasn't so much that she took up all of my time, as it was that I was tired by the time I got home, and I still had to do everyday things to get ready for the next day. I realized that I was a little obsessed with her because she filled a void in my life. I decided that maybe I should start seeing a real person that could respond back to me. It is very easy to become attached to your dog, because they really are like children, except they can't talk. They can make the same mess as a child, with toys everywhere, and they demand so much of your attention. It was time to join the real world and date.

The way to date at that time was using Match.com. It was the hot way to meet people. I did a profile, and the dating began with conversations on the phone. This was not always smooth, because as I was talking on the phone, she was bringing toys for me to throw, which was a distraction. You have to imagine this: you're talking to someone you don't know, trying to lead or participate in a conversation, and there's your dog, standing in front of you with pitiful eyes and toy in mouth. What was I to do but throw the toy? I realized that it was best not to come in talking on the phone or to take any phone calls, until she had been taken out. Did this solve the problem? No, but it did help a little.

I made sure that anyone I was going to meet knew that I had a dog, and we were a package deal. I think some people thought that they could get around this, but they soon found that I was not joking: no Anita without GG. My youngest daughter, as I thought of GG (my daughter hates when I say GG is her sister), did not like men. I realized, over a period of time, that whenever I took her out, if a man spoke to me, she growled, and if a man came to fix the cable or something, she would bark her head off. No, nothing had changed with my development, still no pets. So, when men that worked for the development came, she still had to be out of sight. I would put on loud music to muffle her barks, but I could hear her.

GG put her matchmaking skills to work whenever I had a woman over. It was she and I, so whenever a woman would come over, she would bark, but it didn't have much force to it. The man bark was loud, with her jumping a little off the floor. The woman bark didn't last continuously, like the man bark. With women she would jump on the person, sit between us, and lay her head in my lap, or bring toys for me to throw, and when I didn't respond, she'd sort of shove her toy at the person. She was, I guess, demanding that one of us stop talking and play with her. If the person stayed over, GG was in between us, or sleeping on their head. I mean, some women were like, "Put her in another room," or I would hear my guest talking to her in a rough voice. I will only say that I am not with any of those people. GG knew the best person for me, and she would not let me settle for anyone else, no matter whether I liked the person or not. Yes, it was hard sometimes to choose GG, but now, in hindsight, I know that she was looking out for me

Post 7

Another Year Another Smoke Alarm Battery Change

The months were passing, and there were really no incidents that caused me problems. GG was on the job of being my matchmaker, and I was in a daily routine. All was good. I had forgotten that each new year meant another smoke alarm battery change. One day approaching my door I saw a notice on my front door, I knew it couldn't be good. I went into the house slowly. For some reason, I could feel myself sweating. I hadn't even read the notice, and all of this was happening. I greeted GG half-heartedly and put the notice on the table face down. I would let it wait until I took her out. I bundled her up in her coat and put her in the carrier. I didn't worry about people seeing her anymore. I think I just didn't care. It was cold, so we didn't go far; a short drive to the little shopping mall, and in ten minutes, we were back in the warm car. I drove home like a person taking their last walk before being executed... very slowly. I realized that I might as well get this over with. I'm now trying to understand what I was so afraid of, and I actually can't tell you. When you are doing something wrong, anything out of the ordinary kind of spooks you, because you figure you've been found out. We finally got home, I undressed GG, showered and changed, and got our dinner. I settled in for the night, so much so that I almost forgot about the dreaded notice

I sat at the table and read it. It's smoke alarm time again. I had 7 days before someone was coming in. My thoughts were going faster than I could process them: "What was going on at work that I needed to be there?" What was I going to do with GG? GG was bigger and didn't like to be in her carrier. She barked more loudly now, and her playfulness had gone up a notch – no, make that 10 notches. I sat there for what seemed like an hour, but when I finally came to my senses, only 10 minutes had passed. I tried to go to sleep, but I couldn't, and this time I couldn't blame GG; it was the notice.

I want to tell anyone who has just gotten a puppy and has to work, to plan on not sleeping much. I had been sleep-deprived since getting GG. I got more rest on the train back and forth to work than I did at home. Whenever I fell asleep, I would feel this little paw hitting me in the face. She wanted to play, and it would be 1 o'clock in the morning; she didn't care. She thought that she was being helpful by being my alarm clock, except the time she thought I should get up was nowhere near the 3am I had to get up. Anyway, back to the smoke alarm.

I had a big problem. I couldn't take off work that day because I had a supervisor's meeting. I just had to pray that she would be quiet. The days went by quickly for some reason. It was probably my imagination; before I knew it, the dreaded day had come. I decided to leave her out of the carrier and leave the television in the bedroom on. I left for work, not knowing what was going to happen when I got home. It was a long day at work and the clock didn't seem to move. Finally, it was time to leave work and get the train home. When I got home, I don't know why, but for some reason, I opened the door slowly and walked very slowly up the stairs. My heart was beating fast. I guess that I thought management would be sitting in the living room with GG. When I got to the top of the stairs, I started looking around for GG. I forgot that she was in the bedroom. She was hiding under the bed. I had to coax her out. I did wonder if something had happened because she seemed scared. I held her tight and started our at home play session. She snapped out of her fear, and I forgot all about the smoke alarm check. We went back to our routine and all was good... or so I thought.

It was about 2 weeks later, and again, there was a notice on the front of my door. I wasn't worried this time, because there wasn't anything going on that I needed to be at work for, and I had started working from home. When I got into the house and read the notice, I sat down on the first chair I reached. GG had been discovered, and management wanted to see me. I was pissed at the same time as I was scared, because there were people who had cats. The next day, I went to the management office, and of course, they said they had a policy of no pets, and my dog would have to go. I informed them that there were a number of people who had cats and even dogs. They weren't hearing that. I left without saying yes to giving up GG. I went home and researched the pet policy in all of their developments and discovered that cats weren't allowed either. If they were going to say I had to leave, then what about the people with cats? I wasn't giving up GG, but I wasn't stupid either. I thought it was a race thing.

The next day, there was a knock at the door. I put GG in the bedroom. It was the man in charge of the development. He went on to tell me about the development's pet policy, and I told him about the cats. I threatened to call the newspapers and report their unfair pet policy. While I was threatening him, GG was scratching to get out of the bedroom. I may have been wrong, but don't pretend like other people weren't doing something wrong. We came to an agreement that I would leave, but I had 6 months to find another apartment. He asked me to keep her out of sight, because he didn't want other people getting pets. I agreed. I didn't care what I agreed to. After he left, I wasn't hiding her anymore. The hunt for a pet-friendly apartment was on!

Post 8

Things Pile Up: No Joke

GG was probably 2yrs old and I was stressed. I needed a pet-friendly, reasonably priced apartment for me and GG. You ever try to find a reasonable apartment in New Jersey? Then you understand why I was stressed. I was also trying to date, and GG was turning the people down faster than I could get to know them. This was her job, matchmaker, and she took her job seriously. I had one person come and stay an hour and that was it. What did she do? She showed off with her barking and bringing toys for me to throw. The action that embarrassed me was her squatting and pooping near the person's shoes. I was embarrassed beyond talking. I could only apologize and suggest we do this some other time, since I needed to not only clean my floor but also her butt. I was furious with GG in front of the person, but after the person left and I thought about it, I realized she was telling me a big no. I knew she really didn't like that person because she hadn't pooped in the house except for when I first got her. I started to have telephone dates rather than actual go-out dates. I figured at least I could get to know the person before GG gave her yay or nay. I had six months to find a new apartment and with commuting to New York from New Jersey, which was a two-hour ride each way by train or bus, I was exhausted. My telephone dates helped a lot, because talking to a real person was a lot better than talking to GG, who would look at me with big cute eyes but could not respond in a language I could understand. The people who I met, at least a couple of them, helped a lot by taking me out to look for an apartment on the weekends. I already knew that there was nothing romantic going on, so I ignored GG's shenanigans. I can tell you, as good as a relationship is, having good friends is just as important. We sometimes forget about our friends when we have a relationship but sometimes, we lose our friends because they don't understand that priorities have to change when you're in a relationship. It's sad either way. I spent much of my weekends looking at apartments and it was frustrating. I only looked at pet-friendly apartments, but there were other things to consider since I was alone. I needed to be close to transportation and I had to feel safe. I figured I'd know it when I saw it, but my time was running out. Let me share something strange about my little matchmaker dog. She seemed to know when someone was just a friend and nothing romantic was happening. I know it's weird, isn't it? It could be just that most of the time when someone was taking me apartment hunting or even just going out for a meal they never came into my apartment unless they were going to the bathroom. I guess that made her job easy, them not staying. Finally, I found a pet-friendly apartment with a fireplace. I was beyond happy that I was finally leaving that dog-prejudiced development. GG finally gave the OK for a person.

Post 9

GG: My Matchmaker

WooHoo New Home and New Love. Finally!! I was out of that apartment and no more sneaking around with GG. The new apartment was on the third floor but came with a fireplace. I was ecstatic. I was still having my telephone dates and checking out match.com[1] when I had time. This day and age, how do you meet someone? It's all about the dating apps and fumbling through meeting this person and that one. It's not easy, because there are so many people that misrepresent themselves. Let me tell you a very true story that was told to me by someone I dated. The person I was seeing went to meet a person in a public place and could see her from afar at the designated meeting place. She didn't like what she saw, so she got in her car and drove off. She called the person and told her that something came up and left it like that. I do feel for people who have to go the online dating route but thank God it worked for me. Okay, let me get back on topic.

I saw a posting that I thought was interesting, and I whipped out the fill-in-the-blank document I created for introduction. Wait, follow me closely, it was interesting. In fact, I wondered whether this person was sleeping with someone she shouldn't have been and had two children that she was pretending were her sisters. I would rush home, take GG out, and hit the phone with my good friend. We would laugh and say all kinds of crazy things that we'd made up about this person I'd met on match.com[2]. I was still talking to the person online. Why? There was something about her that intrigued me, not just the sister thing. We talked and talked, and finally I had to ask her about what my thoughts were. She explained that they were indeed her sisters, and how she ended up with them. Talk about egg on the face. We talked as friends for a while, then it was time for the big reveal; we met in person and talked. She was younger than me, so I danced around the age issue for a while.

---

1. http://match.com/

2.   http://match.com/

The more we talked, the more we liked each other, and finally, we started dating and I met her sisters. When I met them, any reservations I had about their relationship to her was dismissed. The being that actually needed to approve was GG.

GG tried some of her tricks, such as sleeping on top of her head, and bringing toys for me to play with to interrupt our conversations. The one thing that GG did that annoyed me was constantly barking whenever someone came over to visit, or just to fix something in the apartment. She didn't do that with her. Life was good. It was very good. GG barks constantly when someone comes into the house, to this day; however, whenever it is a man, she follows them around barking and does her matador dance. The matador dance is when she scrapes her paws on the floor like a bull, and I mean her little feet be moving. I think that maintenance man at the old apartment scared her, and she now shows her dislike of men with barking that doesn't stop until he leaves.

No more match.com[3] for me! We were dating exclusively, and GG liked her, though she did continue to sleep over her head. The one thing that was messed up was losing a friend, because I didn't have the time to sit on the phone 10 times a day anymore. I worked long hours. My days were over 12 hours long, with commuting and taking GG out. I just wasn't as available to my friend, and she resented that. It's a shame when your love life and friendships don't mesh.

I didn't have to hide with GG, so we'd usually go to the park. I'll tell anyone that the way to meet people is to buy a dog. A dog is an icebreaker and conversation piece all rolled into one. You should try it! Get a dog and go to where the dog people are, then let the dog off the leash and just sit there. Someone will start a conversation. All that you need is one person to start the conversation, and all others will follow. You are on your way. You can thank me later for that advice.

Post 10

---

3.   http://match.com/

To Be Or Not To Be

GG and I moved into a new apartment, and I had met someone that she approved of. All was good. GG and I were good. The dating I was doing was exclusive and progressing at a good pace. I'll call my new love K. K worked in the military full-time and was in the process of buying a house when we met. She was also taking care of her two, very young, sisters. We all got along in Willingboro, NJ, the girls loved to play with GG, and I was happy. There is always a storm brewing somewhere, so let me sweep you up in mine.

I hadn't been with kids in a very long time. My daughter was grown, and it was enough to pick up after GG. My heart was heavy when K and I talked about moving in together. The reason was, at this point in my life, with commuting and work, did I really want to raise two little girls? It was hard not to seem cruel, especially knowing the situation that they were in. I had to be honest, with not only myself, but with K: I just couldn't do kids. I'm not going to go any further about that situation, but it's not as cut and dry as you might think. Anyway, once the situation was settled with the girls, and GG and I moved in, another storm started to brew. This time it was how dating and living together are to different animals.

When you date, you put out the best in you, which is sometimes somewhat fake. It happens to all of us. We start being attentive, hanging onto every word the person has to say. You take the time to dress in your nicest clothes. You say and do, not what you want, but what you think that person wants to hear. This is why some relationships don't last; you get tired. Faking is hard work and getting to know someone is harder work. I think that, if we are honest, we all have done it at least once. K and I were no different. We went all-in emotionally. The problems were finding that common ground for balance. I was used to thinking about no one but myself and GG, and she was used to thinking about herself and her sisters. I did certain things for GG, and those things I refuse to budge on. I didn't give up my apartment just in case this didn't work out. I let the lease run out. GG and I were moving into someone else's home, and if things didn't work out, we'd be on the street looking crazy. No, I wasn't taking any chances, especially since we both stopped faking it and were now showing our real selves. There was no more getting dressed up, just to sit around the house. We had to learn compromising, and one thing I can say is that we were in it to win it, because we didn't give up. There were times we'd come close, but never pulled the trigger on our relationship. We were raw and open. The only thing I felt guilty about was leaving GG alone so often. K and I went out on the weekends, leaving GG alone, and I felt guilty.

I would broach the subject of getting her company, but K always shot it down. She wasn't a dog person, and GG was enough for her. Don't get me wrong, she was good with GG, and would walk her and make sure she had food, but she was not a "GG is my daughter" type of person, rather she had a "GG is a dog, and should be treated as such" approach. I ignored that because I know it takes time and patience to change people. The guilt of looking at GG's sad eyes when we went out was heartbreaking. K and I had been together for over 2 years, and again, things were good. Finally, one day I suggested that we just go look at dogs at The Puppy Barn. I was shocked when K said, "Okay." I mean, I was ecstatic, because any other time she'd say, "No!" and I'd leave it alone. A relationship takes compromise. That's why I left it alone, because she contributed a lot for Gg's upkeep and even played with her at times. I know that all of you pet people know the upkeep is expensive, and K never complained.

Post 11

Just Because

GG and I moved in with K, who I was in an exclusive relationship with. We were trying to find common ground, or maybe I should say, a compromise. We were going out on weekends, and GG was left at home alone. I felt guilty, because she wasn't my first priority and I still had to find a balance between taking care of her and my relationship with K. I thought getting another dog might help, at least then she would have company. I would bring up the idea of getting another dog, but K would shoot the idea down. I was excited when I asked and finally got an okay. We went to PetSmart to look at their dogs. There were some cuties, but after hearing that they dealt with puppy mills, I thought we should go to Puppy Barn. Many years ago, I got a golden retriever from them, and my experience was good. Puppy Barn had all kinds of puppies, and I knew I wanted a King Charles or another Shih Tzu, preferably a female.

However, I figured I'd let K pick the dog, just because it was her first experience buying a dog, and I figured she'd be more involved and invested if she thought that this was her own dog. I had no problem with that, I just wanted company for GG; those sad eyes of hers were killing me. So, to Puppy Barn we went. The first dog she picked was a boy, who was lovable and loved to lick you. We named him Rudy, because he seemed like a lover. Rudy had a cold, so the attendant at Puppy Barn told us to let them have a doctor look at him and to come back on Monday. We were on our way to Atlantic City for the day, so Monday was good for us. The ride to Atlantic City was full of excitement, it was full of "Rudy this" and "Rudy that". But I didn't realize that all of the excitement was coming from me. I should have known it was too good to be true, and it was. K had all kinds of doubts. The trip to Atlantic City was no longer a fun trip in the end, and by the time we got back home, Rudy was no longer a reality.

As the days passed, we became tense with each other and I only paid attention to GG, which K hated. I'll be honest, K was - and still is -

jealous of GG, and it was obvious to me. Finally, about a week later, she agreed to get Rudy and bring him home. The ride back to Puppy Barn was full of excitement, and this time I made sure it wasn't just me. But when we got to Puppy Barn and inquired about Rudy, we were told that he had been sold. I almost cried. K saw how upset I was, and suggested we look for another puppy. I let K take the lead, walking around and holding puppies. She seemed to melt with each puppy she held. We walked around twice, looking, and holding. I was still going to let her pick the puppy and name him/her. We kept going back to a stall that had Shih Tzus in it. There must have been about 6 puppies inside, all playing together except one that was curled up by himself in the corner. K picked him up and he started licking her - K fell in love with him. The puppy was a boy, but it was her choice. Puppy Barn checked him out and gave us our going-home package and instructions. We finally had a new addition to our home.

He was cute and fluffy, and seemed to curl right up in my arms during the drive home. I'm bad with time, but I'd say that GG was about 6 years old then. I couldn't wait for her to see her little brother. Our little family was complete in my eyes. We were two gay women, with two dogs and a house; no white picket fence, but we had a patio. We finally got home, and I carried him into the house. GG was on the bed, so I took him over to her to introduce him to her... she looked at him and moved far away from him. I was like, "Okay, let's all sit together and name him," but GG kept staying away. K decided that his name would be Mason. When we looked at him closely, we noticed his eyes were crossed. Maybe all of this was a sign that something was not good. What was worse than his crossed eyes, was the fact that GG refused to acknowledge him at all. Mason would try to snuggle up to her, and she'd move away from him. What did I do? This was just the beginning of Mason's story, the story of a dog from hell.

Post 12

Mason Did What?

I was on my way to having that fantasy we all dream of as children. The marriage, kids, and white picket fence. However, in my case, the marriage was a relationship with a woman, the kids were dogs, and the white picket fence was a cement floor patio. It was all good, nevertheless. I was finally able to get another dog for company for GG. She named him Mason. Mason was a fluffy little crossed eyed dog that deceived my partner with hugs and kisses. GG ignored him; no matter how he tried to cozy up to her, she would just move to the other side of the room and watch him. I wonder if she was waiting for him to touch her toys so she could drag him across the floor like a mop. I thought I got the evil eye for leaving her on the weekends to go out, but the look I got now was worse. Mason didn't do much but sleep and try to snuggle. I made sure I didn't touch him for long when GG was looking because the evil eye was worse than the "why is he here?" look. Every look of hers seemed to get worse than the one before, or maybe it was my imagination. I didn't crate train GG, so I figured that there was no need to do it with Mason, even though my partner K thought we should. Well, we let them have the run of the house while we were at work. This was a big mistake. I would get home first, and every time I walked in the house the mess was worse than the day before. Mason peed everywhere, torn training pads, and chewed furniture legs. It was horrible. I figured out that K was staying at work just so she didn't have to clean up the mess. Why didn't I think of that first? Our relationship was going to hell with arguments about Mason. GG would just look at me with a "who told you to bring him here?" look. I could scream. We took Mason to the vet to get fixed, which I hoped would stop some of his bad behavior. The vet said he was still kind of young for the procedure, but she would do it because he was well endowed. What the blank did that mean? Was she saying he was a baby-making machine or what? I just looked at her with a blank look, not knowing what to say. We slept upstairs with GG. She slept at the end of the bed on top of the covers. We bought Mason a crate after a while because the stress of coming home to a mess was too much. We were going to let him sleep in his crate at night. Mason cried all night, and with me having to get up at 3am for my commute, this made me an unhappy camper. We tried putting him in his crate during the day, but his crying was so loud, we thought someone would call animal control. I mean, he was loud, and it probably seemed louder at 4:45am when I left for the bus. We had a nice, comfortable couch. I mean, those cushions were so soft, your butt sank right in. We had to throw it out because Mason thought it was his fire hydrant. The couch was maybe only 2 years old and K was not happy. Mason had one paw out the door. We then decided not to crate him, but to put up a gate across the kitchen entryway. We were hoping he would not cry if he wasn't confined. Well, one night, we were upstairs watching television when, out of nowhere, Mason was coming up the stairs we had against the bed for GG to get up and down from the bed. To this day, I can't tell you how he got over the fence and up the stairs. I'm only just beginning with Mason's escapades.

Post 13

Not Nice

Mason, as you have read in my previous blog, is a handful. GG hated him, and my partner and I were at our wit's end over what to do with him. There was no leaving him downstairs at night, since he would somehow manage to get upstairs. The messes he would make were unbelievable, or maybe I was tired after my commute to work and back home. We tried to have a routine for him by taking him out as soon as one of us came home; but it seemed that whether he went out in the mornings or evenings, there would still be a mess to clean up. This dog had more poop in him than a dog park. It was unbelievable! For some reason, the neighborhood kids loved him. They always asked about walking him and GG. I decided to help this young lady with her dog-walking business by letting her and a friend walk them. I paid them a few dollars until I discovered they weren't really walking them at all; they would take them to her porch and sit. That was the end of helping the kids with their dog-walking business. I was back walking them in the evenings when I came home. I say me, because my partner would make up all kinds of excuses as to why she had to work late. I know, because in one of our usual Mason arguments, she let it slip out. Can you believe this?! I couldn't. I'm getting up at 3am and getting home at 5pm; and she didn't want to walk or clean up, so she just didn't come home until she was sure I was done. Well, once you say it, there's no way to take it back. Once I knew what she was doing, that came to a stop; and fast. I wasn't having it because Mason was out of control. Well, she topped me by volunteering to go to Afghanistan for a year. I'm not going to say Mason was the only reason, but he did play a part in that decision. I was on my own with these two. I don't know how many of you have dogs, but walking GG and Mason was tactical. The first thing I had to do when taking Mason out was survey the area to make sure there were no people or pets out. The problem came when he saw people that spoke to me. He would try to jump and bite them. If he saw another animal, he would bark like crazy, pulling me and the leash in the direction of the other animal. I would end up holding the leash up high, so his feet were no longer on the ground, they were moving in the air, trying to get to the other animal. GG just tried to stay out of his way. It was a crazy scene. The only way to avoid this kind of problem was if someone were coming down the street, I would walk in the opposite direction. When there were animals or people coming from both directions, I was screwed. We still, to this day, have to survey the area before we can leave the house.

Mason would try to play with GG, but she wasn't having it. He would hit her with his paw, trying to get her to chase him. She would just go sit down in another area. He would push her out of the way when coming from outdoors so he could come in first and then look behind himself to see if she were chasing him. She would just mosey along. The thing Mason did that bothered GG the most was he hid milk bones all through the house. I wondered if he thought a famine was coming and wanted to make sure he had food. GG would watch him hide the milk bones, and wait for a while, and then would go get the milk bone. That would make him so mad.

We realized that leaving him downstairs at night was not going to work, so we would all go up together. Mason would have bothered GG all day; so, when she got to the top of the stairs first, she would bump him with her nose, and he would go tumbling downstairs. He eventually knew what was going to happen, and he'd wait for her to go into the bedroom before he would come upstairs. It was funny, but then again, not funny, because he could have broken something; but I understood GG's frustration, because we were all frustrated with Mason.

Post14

Stress

The tension in the house was at an all-time high. My partner, K, wanted Mason out, and so did GG. I just couldn't do it. K and I were arguing at home, but that wasn't enough, so she'd call me on her way to work to argue some more. It was crazy. Sure, I could have her find a home for him, but I came to need him. You see, when she decided to go to Afghanistan, Mason became a watch dog. He was probably three years old. Mason did not let anyone walk past the house without barking. The person could be two blocks away and he'd start barking, so it was somewhat comforting to have him at home. He was a good watch dog from afar, because as soon as someone saw him, they would see this little Shih Tzu with a big mouth. Mason couldn't leave now, so if K's intention was for me to do something with him, that backfired on her. I know what you are thinking: why not just find him a good home, with kids and an adult who would be at home all day or a senior? I don't know why I was so against it, except that I didn't see anyone keeping him for long, and he'd end up in a shelter somewhere. We paid a good amount of money for him, plus three couches, French doors to keep him blocked in the kitchen, and a crate. We are not rich people, so the expense of Mason was enormous. GG still had very little interaction with him, but he continued to try to get her to play tag with him. K would watch all kinds of dog training shows and nothing worked. He was untrainable. How did I come to that conclusion? Well, K took him to PetSmart for dog training. I didn't attend, and she said he was an embarrassment. Mason wouldn't follow any commands, and he even pooped on the floor. He barked at all the dogs and was a disruption to the class. Untrainable. She was, in so many words, asked not to bring him back, and "maybe he would benefit from one-on-one training?" We just couldn't afford anything else that pertained to Mason. There did come a time when I thought, "Mason has to go." He was costing us a fortune. I was given the cold shoulder by GG, whenever he came near me. What I mean by "cold shoulder" is that I'd call her, and she'd look at me and turn her head. Again, I couldn't get rid of him with my K leaving. What would you have done? I did my best to deal with him and stopped arguing. She was leaving, why should she care? I don't know how many of you take your dogs to the vet, but it's expensive. The vet we use cost $300 just for shots for one of them, so that was doubled. The groomer is $160 for the both of them, and there's no tax deduction for that. I'm telling you this in case any of you are thinking of getting a puppy. I couldn't believe one dog could do so much damage, not just to our home, but to my relationships with K and GG. The biggest problem was that we were both working, and Mason more or less had to teach himself. He was like a latch key kid on his/her own, while his/her parents were at work. GG didn't care for him and was happy being the only dog, so teaching Mason wasn't one of the things she had any interest in doing. I was in unfamiliar territory because I didn't have any of these problems with GG. GG learned quickly how to use the weewee pad and not destroy the house. Actually, while I was at work, she wouldn't eat or drink water; she slept. That was why she was always so energetic because she was well-rested. I realized that not eating and drinking was my punishment for leaving her. When people came to my home, there was no smell. They didn't know I had a dog until the person saw her. Mason, on the other hand, had us buying stock in air freshener companies, we were buying so much of the stuff.

Post 15

Argh, He's Still Here

I'm sure we all who have a dog thinks their dog is special, and I'm not saying Mason isn't special, but he's also a little off. I'm not saying he doesn't have his good moments, because he does. We all have our way of dealing with Mason, like GG pushes him down the steps with her nose. I show him the remote. K, well, the back scratcher is her weapon of choice. Before anyone thinks animal control should have been called, we did not hurt him. He was tapped so lightly that he'd just look up at you and have what looked like a grin on his face.

Post 16

Barking And Jumping

How can one dog cause so much havoc in a family? I experienced none of this behavior from GG. K went to Afghanistan for a little less than a year, which left me and GG against Mason. Mason actually thought he was the man of the house. When it was time for bed, he would get in K's spot in the bed and put his head on the pillow. Can you imagine turning over and knowing that spot should be empty, and opening your eyes to find Mason stretched out? GG, meanwhile, is lying on top of the covers at the foot of the bed like she'd been taught. Mason wasn't having any of the foot of the bed on top of the covers nonsense. I would put him at the foot of the bed, only to wake up and find him lying next to me. Sometimes I'd look over at him on his back with his paw straight up in the air snoring away. I couldn't get a break. GG was not only giving me the evil eye, but now she was ignoring me when I called her. What could I do? Stay up all night to keep putting him at the foot of the bed?

I left for work before 5am in the morning, so I couldn't take them out until I got home. I had read that, when you leave your dogs, you shouldn't acknowledge them, you should just walk out the door. When you come home, you then acknowledge your dog as soon as you enter. Well, when I left, he would start barking and jumping on the door. I felt sorry for my neighbor because, every morning that I went to work, he had to listen to Mason's mouth. I sometimes would stand outside the door to see if he stopped once I locked the door. Nope, Mason would still be jumping and barking. I wonder how long after I left before he realized I wasn't coming back. They say girls mature faster than boys. I guess that goes for dogs too.

When I came home and opened the door, I would acknowledge GG first and then Mason, but most of the time I had to bypass Mason because he would have knocked GG to the side so he could be picked up first. I would take them out as soon as the hello's were done, and of course the mess was cleaned up. The problem in the summer was people were out. This meant I had to spend as much time trying to dodge people as walking them. When I had no choice but to pass a person, Mason would slow down and start running in circles, so now I was tangled in the leash, and GG would just sit there looking at me as if to say, "You got him so you deal with him."

The other crazy thing about walking him was that he seemed to know where every dog lived. We would be on the sidewalk walking, when he got near a house with a dog he would creep up to their door and stop waiting for a dog to show him/herself. Sometimes, I would have to drag him from the front of houses. I think people felt sorry for me and tried to go the opposite direction or keep their dog from in front of the window or door. I was just embarrassed by his antics. Mason and the neighborhood cats were also an issue. I kept the front door open and the storm door locked so they could look out. The cats would walk in front of the door or window and just stop, which started Mason barking and going in circles. I'd just sit and watch this on a number of occasions. When we were out walking and I had no choice but to walk in front of a cat, Mason would look in the opposite direction of the cat and pretend he didn't see the cat. I know if I saw the cat, he saw the cat too. He's all bark and nothing else. I don't like cats, and on one occasion when walking GG and Mason there was a cat across the street chasing a squirrel. The cat stopped trying to get the squirrel when he saw Mason, and he put his tail up. I was like oh shit, what do I do?' I had no choice but to keep walking toward home. The cat was taking a few creeping steps in our direction and stopped. I prayed all the way home.

Post 17

A New Home

Cats just can't stand Mason. When we pass them, they look at us with their sneaky, beady eyes, and with tails in the up position. Mason, on the other hand, pretends not to see the cats by turning his head in the opposite direction. There have been times when a cat has been sleeping under a bush outside, and Mason decided he had to go under that bush. When this happens, I pull him back on the leash while he barks and the cat screeches. The squirrels outside in front of the house are also enemies of Mason. The squirrels stand on their hind legs in front of the door, which drives Mason crazy. Mason runs back and forth in front of the door, barking. To me, the squirrels are quite bold to stand there like that. Mason, as you can tell, just has a personality that animals love to hate.

One day, K called from Afghanistan to tell me that she wanted us to buy a house with the money she was making. I was tasked with managing the money and finding a realtor. I found a realtor and started looking online for a house in Florida. We didn't want to deal with snow or excessive cold in our old age, neither did we want to do stairs. Do you know the effort that goes into walking upstairs? When you get old, it's a little too much effort, though doctors will call it exercise. I call it a BENGAY hurt. I saw online that in Florida, there were a lot of houses being sold through a short sale. A short sale happens when the owner is underwater, and the lender agrees to take less than the amount still owed on the house. Banks are not in the real estate business, and therefore they will sell houses at a discount. Six years ago, Florida had plenty of short sale houses. I was warned that short sale houses are sometimes ruined by a disgruntled owner. I had a great realtor who looked out for us. There were pitfalls I needed to be aware of, such as Chinese drywall. Chinese drywall was used in building some houses in Florida because it was cheap. The downside to Chinese drywall is that it smells like rotten eggs.

My realtor informed me of which places were good ones and which were money pits. She found us a place in a great neighborhood with not too many kids. You have to remember that all this was done over the phone and emails. I didn't go down even once to see the place. I trusted my realtor, and hoped I did the right thing.

K finally came home, and 2 years later, we drove by way of I-95 to Florida with GG and Mason. We were beyond excited to see the Florida house. We mapped our trip, taking in consideration stopping for water, bathroom breaks and eating. We stopped about every 3 hours. When we got to Florence, SC - the halfway point for us - we stopped and stayed at La Quinta. I liked La Quinta because it didn't smell like animals and it was clean. There was an area out back to walk them. Mason, of course, was an embarrassment. If he heard any noise in the hallway, he started barking and wouldn't stop. It was a hotel, so there was always noise in the hallway. When we took him out, we had to try to find an area where there weren't any dogs or people. That all took time and patience, which we were short on. We were tired. At least they tolerated the drive well.

When you get to the development, you have to turn right past the cows. Yep, there were cows at the beginning of the development. Finally, we got to our new home. It was very nice, more than we expected. One day, while walking GG and Mason, we decided to walk to the corner store, which was past the cows. When Mason saw the cows, he started barking and running back and forth; his usually antics. What happened next blew my mind. The cows starting moving toward the fence where we were. They were just looking at Mason, and as we walked, the cows walked sideways along the fence with us. It was a sight to see. I didn't have a camera with me the one time I needed it. I've surmised that maybe Mason is a Dr. Dolittle, an animal that can attract, gather, and be a leader of other animals. Okay, maybe that's a bit much.

The house has a fenced-in patio and pond out back. There are always ducks in the pond. The Sandhill Cranes can walk to the fenced-in patio, which, once again, drives Mason crazy. They come and just look at him, running back and forth, barking. On one of these occasions, one of the Sandhill Cranes came up to the patio fence and put a hole in it trying to get at him. We grabbed them and ran into the house. GG had started to bark more often. I figured she thought that was the way for her to get attention. GG would start to bark when Mason started. It was like the wild kingdom. There are plenty of dogs in the development that are probably better controlled than Mason because you don't hear them.

Post 18

Personalities

I wanted to talk to you about the difference between GG and Mason. I wasn't a dog person always, and I can't say exactly how it happened. I know I don't like cats, because to me they are sneaky animals with beady eyes. No offense to the cat lovers, it's just my preference. I've had three dogs in my lifetime, and they were two different breeds: lab and Shih Tzu. The first dog, the lab, I left when my relationship ended. GG, my first Shih Tzu, I got because I was lonely and needed company, and Mason, my other Shih Tzu, I got because I thought GG needed company. I've wondered how many people get dogs to soothe some kind of paternal emotion they have, since having a dog is like having a child that can't talk. I have also come to realize that some dogs are more intelligent than others, and their personalities can be quite different. It has nothing to do with their breeds, but it has more to do with their personalities, like people. There are book-smart people and people who need a little more patience for them to get it. I have found with GG and Mason that there are teachable dogs, and some dogs that need waaaayyyyyy more patience than I have. GG took a weekend to learn to use a training pad, while it took Mason four years, three couches, two baby gates, a crate, and french doors before he got the message. GG is a clean freak. When she poops or her water is low, she comes over and barks like crazy until you get up and follow her to whatever needs to be taken care of. Mason couldn't care a bit about cleaning up anything after him. GG tries to keep her food on her mat, while Mason will drag his food to any corner to hide it for when we can't afford to feed him. When GG gets tired of walking, she will step down on her leash to say, "That's it for me, take me home." Mason wants to keep walking so he can disturb the neighbors with his barking. GG isn't afraid of thunder, while Mason is afraid of rain, snow, thunder, and lightning. You get the picture—he only likes sunshine and warm weather. Mason is on medication because of his anxiety. I didn't have to take GG to any pet training for her to understand commands. Mason was taken to and put out of a training class. I haven't figured out if Mason is a protector or just figures barking should take care of everything. There have been a couple of occasions when I have been walking them, and a big dog had gotten out of his/her yard. On one of those occasions, GG started to fight with the dog, and on another occasion, she just stood there hoping—like me—that someone would come get this dog. On both occasions, Mason just stood and barked was no protection whatsoever. I am not saying GG doesn't have bad habits, because she does like tearing up training pads when she doesn't get her way. GG hardly barked before Mason came; it was like she discovered that barking gets attention once they met. I do know that she got all her bad habits from Mason. I kept Mason because his barking gave me a sense of security while K was in Afghanistan. Mason does have his good points, but right now I can't think of any. Really. He did grow out of being cross-eyed and can be lovable at times. The point is, just like kids, these two are as different as can be. Think about a boy and girl and how different they really are in personalities. When you compare dogs and kids, is there really that much of a difference? I look at my floor and there are toys all over the place from GG and Mason playing, and when my grandkids come over, my floor has this same look, except I can have my grandkids pick up after themselves. My final thought on this is that GG and Mason are as different as a boy and girl, and dogs are about the same as children.

Post 19

The Man

I sometimes wonder if Mason thinks he is a human because he stands on his hind legs a lot. He is the only male with three women, and there are times when he thinks it's all about him. An example is when it's hot, he lays in front of the fan, thinking of only his comfort. He pushes GG out the way when they come in from outside because he wants to be first in. It's all about him. Then when he has weather-related anxiety, if we want peace, we had better all get in the bed while he's going through his episode. I'm counting GG with K and I because she is a female. Mason's ways definitely remind me of some men. Some men have limited consideration and a me-first attitude. Here are more reasons why I can compare him to some men. He likes to sleep on a pillow next to one of us, but it doesn't stop there. He has to stretch out. I mean, stretch out like you have no room to lay flat. You have to lay on your side. I can hear K some nights pleading with him to move over. Mason wants to be in charge of GG, like he wants her to chase him, and when their food is put down, he likes to eat it first and leave GG only what he doesn't want. When GG happens to eat first or he decides he wants more after she starts eating, he tries to sneak up behind her to snatch her food. K and I watch as he saunters behind our chair to come up behind her. It is funny because he actually thinks he's doing something. We can dress him in different outfits and he doesn't mind, but GG? She's not having it. She somehow gets the clothes off, or she will just lie there like a lump of clay. One day, while K was in Afghanistan, Mason got out when I cracked the door to get the mail. I had on my pajamas because it was a lazy day for me. A UPS truck drove by the house and Mason took off behind it. The UPS truck made a left turn and Mason was on the truck's tail. I'm running down the street in my pajamas and slippers yelling, "Mason!" Of course, he didn't stop. I haven't run in years, but I knew as much of a headache as he is, I couldn't explain Mason getting out and chasing the UPS truck and me not running after him. I ran out of gas chasing him for a block and a half. Okay, it wasn't far, but to me at that time it was like a marathon. There were people out looking at me running down the street like a crazy person, however, when they realized it was Mason I was chasing, they understood. You see, Mason has gotten out before, but instead of me, it was K who was in her pajamas falling all over the yard out front trying to catch him. He'd let her get close and then take off in the other direction. She had slippers on, so when he would cut to the opposite direction and she tried to catch him, she'd fall on her butt. It was funny, but now that it was me being embarrassed, it was no longer funny. Our whole neighborhood knows of Mason because he is so loud that they can't help but notice him. The other reason they know Mason is because when one of us is walking them, he is usually pulling you down the street while he tries to go after a squirrel. The day I was looking like an idiot running down the street ended when the UPS truck stopped and Mason stopped running. I think he realized he was not at his home because he was looking all around. When I finally got to Mason and picked him up, he was shaking. I guess he was scared. I didn't care that he was scared because here I was in the street in my pajamas. I know he didn't understand, but I used a few choice words on him from the time I picked him up until we got home. I tell you, Mason is going to get us killed. GG is nothing like him. If she were, I'd be crazy. I mean, she did have her moments, like wanting to play all the time until I'd have to go sit in my car to have some peace of mind. She has more sense than Mason, and she doesn't follow him when he's up to his antics. There is an opening where the gate and the gate door come together. Mason will go out the opening and run around to the front door and bang on the door. GG just stands there. When we got him, we used to open one of the car doors, and he'd jump in, thinking he was going for a ride. When we brought him back, GG would be standing at the door, and as soon as Mason was put down, she'd jump on him. I guess she was trying to tell him something, but it took a long time for him to learn.

Post 20

Finishing Up

I will start with K because he pulled the wool over her eyes from the beginning. K was not a dog person at all until I convinced her that GG needed company. I let her pick the dog so she would feel close to him/her. Mason was lying in a corner by himself while his siblings were all playing together. That should have told her something, but with her being a novice around dogs, and me not wanting to interfere, I didn't say anything. Mason was sort of cute with his cross-eyes and fuzziness. K's love for Mason didn't come easy.

She wanted him out when he pooped on the floor and peed on the couch. We argued. She wanted him out when he barked all night. We argued. She wanted him out when he had anxiety and would run all over the house like every room was his bathroom. We argued. She wanted him out when he embarrassed her and got put out of PetSmart dog training. We argued. She wanted him out when she had to spend money to buy three couches, a crate, French doors to block the kitchen, and dog gates. We argued. I know you're wondering how it is that he's still here. He is still here because she went to Afghanistan, and I knew Mason would bark whenever someone came near the house. That is the reason, and the only reason, he is still here. Mason is now seven years old, and 2,555 days later, he's finally got it.

K has come to love him and find him adorable. The biggest problem now is her begging and pleading with him to move over, since he gradually weaseled his way up to the head of the bed so he can share her pillow. There is also the fact that he ignores us when we talk to him. We call his name, and he looks at us and turns his head. We can call him again and again, and he will just ignore us. The only way to get him to respond is clapping your hands or making some kind of noise. Mason still stares at walls, which is a little strange to me. He stares at walls now, even when the sun is shining. He is a dog that loves sunshine and warm weather. If there's rain, thunder, lightning, or snow, his anxiety starts, and he's off into doggy mind land. The main thing is that, after all the arguments, money spent, begging, and pleading, she loves him now. It was rough getting to this point, but we made it.

GG couldn't stand Mason when we first brought him home. She would give me the evil eye if I touched him. When Mason came into a room, she'd leave the room. GG would just look at K and me when we argued as if to say, "You brought him here. I didn't ask for him." I think, after trying to get her to be motherly to him, Mason gave up, and started trying to annoy her. Why do I say that? He'd go and hit her and steal her food and play with her toys. He'd hide Milk-Bones, and still does. Mason would do things and then sit innocently while we tried to figure out who did what. When Mason would go upstairs at night, GG would push him down the stairs and keep going into the bedroom. It was funny at first, but not so funny when we realized he could break a leg and cost us more money. It took her at least five out of seven years of Mason being here for GG to get used to his presence. She does her matador shuffle when she's tired of him bothering her. The matador shuffle is her moving each of her paws like a matador in a bull-fighting ring. When she does that, it's on, and Mason had better watch out. Mason still thinks he should be first, but I show GG love first. I can't say that she loves him, but she tolerates him. Mason's main job now is to keep GG moving.

Post 21

Life is Good

I reside in the Tampa, Florida area with GG, Mason, and my spouse. I served in Army for 6 years and retired from a government agency and she retired her from full-time National Guard. We lived in Willingboro, New Jersey before making the car trip to the sunshine state. Our lives with GG and Mason have been eventful and at times indescribable. I cherish each day she is with me.

I've learned people give up too quickly on relationships these days because they are work. You have to see it through those dark times to see light again. You will know which person is worth going through the dark times with. Your heart will tell you who's worth it.

We've been in Florida for 2 years now and GG just turned 19 years old. She's old and stubborn as ever. Our family is good. It took a lot to get here, but it was worth it. GG finally tolerates Mason and he's calmed down. GG taught me patience, more patience and patience on top of that! Get a dog. You won't be sorry. They bring so much joy, you can't even imagine.

GG is now 19 and Mason 13 years old.

Birthday Girl

GG

Mason

Disclaimer

I have tried to recreate events, locales, and conversations from my memories of them. In order to maintain their anonymity in some instances I have changed the names of individuals and places, I may have changed some identifying characteristics and details such as physical properties, occupations, and places of residence.

Copyright 2020

Becca Day – Book Cover Designer

Printed by Anita Powell
First Printing, 2020
Anita Powell-Publisher
Riverview, Florida

Don't miss out!

Visit the website below and you can sign up to receive emails whenever Anita Powell publishes a new book. There's no charge and no obligation.

https://books2read.com/r/B-A-RPAM-GZITB

BOOKS2READ

Connecting independent readers to independent writers.